A Far-Fetched Story

A FAR-FETCHED STORY

BY **KARIN CATES**

PICTURES BY **NANCY CARPENTER**

Greenwillow Books
An Imprint of HarperCollins Publishers

Library of Congress Cataloging-in-Publication Data
Cates, Karin.
A far-fetched story / by Karin Cates;
illustrated by Nancy Carpenter.
    p.   cm.
"Greenwillow Books."
Summary: With a hard winter on the way,
Grandmother uses her family's rags and
stories to create a cozy quilt.
ISBN 0-688-15938-9 (trade).
ISBN 0-688-15939-7 (lib. bdg.)
[1. Quilts—Fiction. 2. Grandmothers—Fiction.]
I. Carpenter, Nancy, ill. II. Title.
PZ7.C268797 Far 2002   [E]—dc21   2001016152

2   3   4   5   6   7   8   9   10   First Edition

A note about the artwork: The paintings for
A Far-Fetched Story are done in pen and ink
with watercolor on Arches 90 lb. hot-press
watercolor paper. Each family member's
far-fetched tale, as well as a few other
illustrations, are also pen-and-ink drawings
with watercolor that have been color copied
onto transfer paper and ironed onto white
linen. I used a sewing machine and colored
thread to sew additional lines and add details
to the linen paintings.   —Nancy Carpenter

To the mothers
Helen Harlan Wulf
&
Oleta Woodward Cates
—K. C.

To Grandma Sandy
and Grandpa Bob
—N. C.

Early one autumn, long ago and far away, the woodpile was higher than the windowsills. But even so, there was not enough firewood to suit Grandmother.

"Look!" she said. "A whole handful of spiders moved into the kitchen last night. That's a sure sign that a long, hard winter is coming soon."

Grandmother sighed and looked at her grandson. That boy had been making a nuisance of himself all morning. So Grandmother asked him to go to the woods and gather just one more armful of firewood.

The boy hurried off down the hard dirt footpath that led from the house into the darkness of the old woods. He had always believed that a lone wolf lived deep in the woods, and now here was a chance to spy that wolf for himself.

When the boy returned home, he had not one single stick of firewood, and his shirt was in shreds.

"Where is my firewood? And what in the world happened to your shirt?" asked Grandmother.

"A wolf!" cried the boy. "It tore my shirt with its terrible, pointed fangs. It made me forget all about the firewood. I barely escaped with my life!"

"Well, that's a far-fetched story!" said Grandmother. "It's a pity but it can't be helped, and I'm afraid we'll have to burn your shirt for firewood."

"Oh, please, no!" begged the boy. "It's my favorite shirt."

"I know, dearie, but a long, hard winter is coming."

And, slap-bang, Grandmother threw the striped rag into the empty wood box where she liked to keep one extra armful of firewood for emergencies.

Then she said, "Where is your sister? I bet that girl can get one last armful of firewood."

So the girl skipped off to gather firewood. She had known for a long time that a deer had been trampling and even sleeping in the tall weeds behind the old tool shed, and she had been longing to feed it from her very own hand.

But when the girl returned home, she had not
one stick of firewood, and the hem of her dress
was raggedy as if it had been nibbled all around.

"Where is my firewood? And what in the world
has happened to your pretty dress?" asked
Grandmother.

"A deer!" cried the girl. "First it ate my apple, and then it tried to eat my dress. It made me forget all about the firewood. I barely escaped with my life!"

"Well, that's a far-fetched story!" said Grandmother. "It's a pity but it can't be helped, and I'm afraid we'll have to burn your dress for firewood."

"Oh, please, no!" begged the girl. "It's my favorite dress."

"I know, dearie, but a long, hard winter is coming."

And, slap-bang, Grandmother threw the flowered rag into the wood box.

Then she asked both children, "Where is your mother? I wonder if she could get that one last armful of firewood."

So the mother wandered off to gather firewood.

And when she returned home, she had not one stick of firewood, and her gown was unraveling into great lengths and loops of blue and red and black and golden threads.

"Where is my firewood? And what in the world has happened to you?" asked Grandmother.

"Swans!" cried the mother. "They surrounded me. They plucked at my gown, and I myself went spinning round and round. They made me forget all about the firewood. I barely escaped with my life!"

"Well, that's a far-fetched story!" said Grandmother. "It's a pity but it can't be helped, and I'm afraid we'll have to burn this whole tangle for firewood."

"Oh, please, no!" begged the mother. "It's my favorite gown."

"I know, dearie, but a long, hard winter is coming."

And, slap-bang, Grandmother threw the paisley rag into the wood box.

Then she turned to the two children again. "Where is your father? We really must have just one more armful of firewood."

So the father strode off to gather firewood.

When the father returned home, he had not one stick of firewood, and his shirt was full of great clawlike holes.

"Where is my firewood? And what in the world has happened to your shirt?" asked Grandmother.

"A bear!" cried the father. "It tried to steal
my shirt with its terrible claws. It made me forget
all about the firewood. I barely escaped with my life!"

"Well, that's a far-fetched story!" said Grandmother. "It's a pity but it can't be helped, and I'm afraid we'll have to burn your shirt for firewood."

"Oh, please, no!" begged the father. "It's my favorite shirt."

"I know, dearie, but a long, hard winter is coming."

And, slap-bang, Grandmother threw the plaid rag into the wood box.

"We really do need just one more armful of firewood." She looked all around in a determined way. "Where is the baby?" she asked.

The baby was in the backyard picking up little sticks, and throwing down little sticks, and picking up little sticks, and throwing down little sticks. But soon she began to follow something soft and jumpy.

When Grandmother finally found the baby, she was wearing only her diaper and a long flyaway sash. Her little dress was missing.

"Where in the world have you been?" cried Grandmother.

"Rabbits!" said the baby.

"And what in the world happened to your beautiful dress?" asked Grandmother.

"Rabbits!" said the baby.

"And how did you manage to untie your sash all by yourself?" asked Grandmother.

"Rabbits!" said the baby.

"Rabbits!" repeated Grandmother. "Well, that's a far-fetched story if I ever heard one." She shook her head at the long, snaky, polka-dotted sash. "It's a pity but it can't be helped, and I'm afraid we'll have to burn this useless sash for firewood," she said.

"No!" said the baby.

"I know, dearest, but a long, hard winter is coming."

And, slap-bang, Grandmother tossed the polka-dotted rag into the wood box.

Grandmother began to pace back and forth. What a pretty mess this was! A jumble of rags instead of the neat pile of extra firewood she had wanted. And a kitchen full of spiders. And look!

A field mouse scurried through a crack under the door as if it knew, too, that a long, hard winter was coming. And right on the tips of its hind feet, the first breath of cold air rushed inside.

"We'll have to burn these rags tonight!" said Grandmother.

But the minute she picked up one of the rags, her fingers seemed to caress it as if she had found some kind of treasure. The fabric was so soft, the colors were so bright! She held a little piece of rag against her cheek, and it felt as comforting as a kiss.

Suddenly Grandmother plunked herself down beside the wood box and began to rummage around among all the rags. Then she took a pair of scissors and began to cut and snip and trim. When she had finished cutting, she threaded several needles with brightly colored threads and began to stitch and stitch and stitch.

Soon she had made something as long and wide
as a bed and as thick and warm as a coat. It made
a different kind of warmth from firewood. It made
the kind of warmth that lasts forever, instead of
disappearing as burning firewood will do.

"There!" said Grandmother. "A far-fetched story
quilt! And just in time, too."

The quilt was so large and cozy, it kept the
whole family as warm as toast and as safe as fairy
tales all through the long, hard winter, which
came just as Grandmother said it would.

THE END